Strings Attached

By

Carla D E Godfrey

Strings Attached

Copyright © Carla Godfrey 2022

The right of Carla Godfrey to be identified as the author of this work has been asserted by her in accordance with the Copyright, Designs and Patents Act 1988

2020

Part one

Chapter One

'I'm home!!' Anna Cartley took her coat off and quickly removed her high heels, it was eerily quiet; they must all be out. 'Hello?!' She called out again...suddenly, she thought she heard giggling and then someone shushing them. Frowning, she made her way upstairs. 'Hello? Anyone home?' Suddenly, she was met by her husband coming out of the bedroom in a dressing gown; he looked visibly shocked to see her.

'Oh! Hi! I-I thought that you were going to be out all afternoon!'

She just glared at him in stony silence, slowly, she pushed the bedroom door open to find a woman half their ages sitting bolt upright, naked in their bed and looking very sheepish. The blood pounded in her ears as her entire world fell apart, slowly; she turned round and rushed back down the stairs and out the door, not even bothering to listen to her husband's feeble excuses.

****

'Oh my Darling! I'm so sorry!'

Anna stared into her glass, 'I knew things were bad between us Jen...I just didn't realise *how* bad!'

'Oh no! Don't you *dare* do that!'

'Do what?'

Her friend crossed her arms. 'Make excuses for him!'

'I'm not but there isn't just me to think about...there are the kids!'

'Well, they're not kids any more are they?'

'Well...you know what I mean!'

'What happened?'

'Bex and Jerry arrived together and tore him to shreds.'

'Good!'

'What do you mean "good?" He's still their father!'

'Who showed no respect for any of you whatsoever!'

Anna just stared into space; she felt numb and tired, she couldn't cry any more either - she had just had enough.

'Anyway!' Her friend looked at her watch. 'Look, I feel terrible...'

'Don't be stupid! You go!'

'Are you sure? I can stay for another...'

'*No*...You've got a life of your own, I'll be fine.'

'Sure?'

'Yes! I'll just finish this.'

'Well…alright!' Her friend smiled. 'Just don't get drunk on proposition the barman!'

'I don't know! Might get lucky!' They both laughed.

'Bye Darling!'

'Bye!' Anna watched her go and then stared into her glass.

'Can I get you another?'

Anna turned to see a fresh faced, handsome man who could be no more than thirty smiling at her, she looked around her and then turned back to him. 'Who? Me?'

He shrugged. 'Either you or your invisible friend next to you.'

'Oh *very* funny!'

'So?'

'Look, I'm having a bit of a rough time and I'm in no mood to be made fun of thank you so go back to your little friends, be a man and tell them the dare's off or whatever you kids do these days...'

He frowned slightly. 'I'm here on my own actually, and I don't have any agenda, I just want to buy you a drink.'

'Oh please! I could be your mother!'

'I highly doubt that.'

'Oh really? How old are you then?'

'Thirty-two.'

She raised her eyebrows in surprise. '...And how old do you think I am?'

'Late thirties? Early forties at a push...'

She laughed, 'Not bad, and flattery will get you everywhere.'

He grinned. 'Was I close?'

'I'm hanging on to my early forties by a thread...two years to be precise.'

'Well you don't look it.'

'Well thank you...you're very sweet.'

'May I have the honour of knowing your name?'

'So formal! It's Anna.'

'Jeremy.'

'Pleased to meet you Jerry!' He flinched and she grinned. 'Not a fan of "Jerry" then?'

'Not since discovering the cartoon Tom & Jerry no!'

She laughed. 'Get teased at school for it did you?'

'How did you guess? The worst part of it was there actually was a Tom in my class!'

'Friend?'

'No, he used to beat me up; we were literally "Tom & Jerry" except "human Tom" used to be more successful!'

'A "rite of passage" for every boy!'

'Gee...thanks!'

Anna was already beginning to feel a lot better, she looked into his eyes and found something she hadn't seen for a long time; warmth...genuine warmth.

'Shall I get us a bottle?'

'Oh I really shouldn't...'

'Why? Are you driving?'

'No...

'Right! A bottle it is!'

'Don't you have to show ID?' She giggled.

He feigned annoyance. 'As you are a woman I shall overlook that callous, humiliating remark!'

'You're lucky enough to still be asked for ID!'

'Hey! Stop that!'

'So...Jeremy...what do you do?'

'I am a curator in an art gallery.'

She stared at him. 'OK...wasn't expecting that! Which gallery?'

'The one round the corner.'

'I *love* that place! It's so authentic and relaxing!'

'Yes, exactly!'

She smiled. 'So... you're the one responsible for all those beautiful paintings!'

'Careful! You make me sound like I painted them!'

'Busy boy then!'

He laughed. 'Anyway...what about you? What do you do?'

'Oh I...I have my own...well...fashion company...'

Jeremy choked and stared at her. 'Hang on...you wouldn't be Anna Martins by any chance would you?'

'Guilty as charged...my maiden name.'

'You are *kidding* me!'

'No!'

'Wow! Your company makes some pretty decent stuff!'

'Why thank you.'

He stared at her with admiration. 'Wow! Good for you!'

'It just started as little doodles in my bedroom one day and then grew into something else.'

"Well...listen to me...I don't who your husband is but an idiot doesn't begin to describe what he is.'

'Didn't your mother ever tell you it was rude to listen into other people's conversations?'

'Probably! Can't remember!'

She actually laughed. 'Cliché and touché, but thank you...something I needed to hear.' She looked at her watch. 'I'd best think about getting back.'

'OK!' They both got up to leave, he reached across her just as she was getting her handbag, got his arm caught up in the strap and pulled it away from her, it fell to the floor. 'Oh shit!' He bent down and hastily grabbed the things that had fallen out. 'I am so sorry!'

She bent down, grinning although she wasn't sure why. 'Oh that's alright!'

'Here! I haven't pinched your purse so don't worry!'

'Yes but then again you *would* say that wouldn't you?'

'Feel free to check!'

'No, I trust you!'

'Really?'

'Don't worry, rest assured I shall call the police the moment I discover otherwise.'

'Fair enough! Just give me enough notice to arrange a fake passport!'

She laughed. 'Agreed.'

It was dark when she headed outside so she hailed a cab, as it pulled away, she turned back to see him watch it leave. Slowly, she opened her bag, everything was still there, including her purse with cards and money, suddenly, she spotted a piece of paper; she opened it to see it had his name and number on it.

Chapter Two

Jeremy was busy entering data into the computer, every now and then he stopped to think about Anna, she was so sophisticated, fancy someone treating her the way her ex-husband did! He bet she hadn't had any fun in a while - he would have to show her.

****

'How are you Mum?'

Anna smiled as her twenty-two year old daughter greeted her. 'Oh my darling! It's so nice to see you!'

'Well, it's the weekend...I just thought I'd pop in.'

'Oh you don't have to worry about me...'

'Don't be stupid! I still can't believe Dad has done this to you!'

Anna slowly pushed a hand through her daughter's hair. 'Well...to be fair darling, I think it was on the cards...'

'*Really?* We didn't notice anything!'

'Well, no, we kept it hidden from you two.'

'You didn't have to do that Mum.'

She smiled sadly. 'I'm your mum; it's my job to protect you.'

'Not *all* of the time! Look, Mum, after what Dad did to you, you deserve to have some fun alright? Just think of yourself for a change!'

****

Late that evening, Anna sat on the sofa, staring at the piece of paper with his number on it, she bit her lip. Oh for god's sake Anna! Get a grip! He's not that far off half your age! Do you want to be known as a cougar? She reached for the bottle of wine and poured herself another glass. On the other hand...why should it always be men who are allowed to date women half their age? She picked up the receiver and then put it down again - slowly, she thought about her husband and that other woman - once again she grabbed the phone and dialled the number.

'This is really nice!'

'Yes! Makes a change!'

It was a lovely, hot sunny day and Anna had decided to meet Jeremy in the park, they sat on the bench with take away ice-coffees, looking out at the pond.

'I suppose it's hardly the "date" you had in mind!'

'What's that supposed to mean?'

She shrugged. 'I'm guessing you would fancy a night out to a club or something rather than this!'

He laughed. '...And that was very true when I was eighteen - but it's catching up with me these days!'

'Oh please! How old are you?'

'Well...thirty-two isn't *that* young!'

'Are you *trying* to be insulting?!'

'No, but it's clearly back firing!'

She shook her head and smiled, looking out at the water. 'You know, when my husband left me; I really felt past it.'

'*Past it??*'

'Yeah!'

'Why on *earth* would you think that?'

'Well... a woman approaching her mid-forties...two almost grown up kids - hardly attractive is it?'

'Nor is a bunny boiler who wants to get married after only a couple of months!'

'Now THAT'S not exaggerating is it?'

'No…seriously! 'She laughed and he smiled. 'Look, you've had a rough time, your confidence has taken a severe knock...but I think you're lovely!'

'You wouldn't say that if you knew what I looked like first thing in the morning!'

'Is that an invitation?!'

She laughed again. 'Seriously! I'd scare you!'

'I think I could handle it!'

'You're barely older than my kids!'

'Well at least I'm not younger! That's when you should be worrying!'

'Do you manage to put a positive spin on everything?'

'I try to! It gets me through the day!'

'Oh? I sense a chink!'

'Well...it's not a chink as such but when your mother is trying to set you up with every available woman in the area it does get tiring!'

'Ah! I thought so! So...what's wrong with these girls then?'

He shrugged. 'Nothing *per se*...They just don't do it for me...their conversation is *exactly* what you would expect...the whole thing is cliché.'

'What? Discussing the future and make up?'

'Amongst other things!'

Anna grinned. 'Well...it's only natural to size you up to see if you're husband material.'

'Clearly!' Jeremy sipped his drink. 'I'm not a commitment-phobe, I just don't want to go at a million miles an hour and I want it to be with the right woman.'

'I think that's very mature and fair.'

Suddenly a light, cool breeze swept around them and they looked out at the pond and smiled, enjoying each other's company.

****

'So...will you let me take you to dinner?'

'McDonald's?'

'Well...I was thinking somewhere slightly more up market but I'm game if you are!'

She laughed. 'I'll let you take me if you promise to let me pay half!'

'Absolutely not!'

'Well...the taxi then!'

'Deal! I'll make sure it's a long journey!'

'You do that and you're *definitely* paying you free loader!'

He laughed. 'Point taken!'

'So...when exactly were you planning to "fleece" me then?'

'I was thinking Saturday night around seven?'

'That's very specific!'

'Hardly! "Saturday at ten minutes past seven precisely" is specific!'

She grinned. 'Fair point.'

'So?'

'It's a date!'

****

She nervously looked in the mirror and wondered if she was now too old for the "little black dress" routine. Not that it was *that* short. Oh well, it was too late to change now, she had only just done her make up. Suddenly, the doorbell went, after a last look, she grabbed her handbag and went downstairs.

His eyes widened as she answered it. 'Wow! You look...'

'Mutton dressed as lamb?'

'Absolutely not! You look great!'

She blushed as she felt the adrenaline which also unsettled her slightly. 'Well, thanks! So...where are you taking me?'

'McDonald's alright?' She stared at him and he laughed. 'Oh god! You think I'm being serious! As if!'

'Well...I don't like to assume! When did you finish high school again?'

'Ha! Ha! This is going to be fun!

They arrived at the restaurant and were shown to a table. Anna smiled. 'Very nice! I'm impressed!'

'It's free if you do the "get up slowly from your table and run tactic!"

'What in these heels?'

'Oh don't worry! I'll be fine!'

She laughed.

He smiled at her. 'You have a great laugh!'

'Flattery will get you no-where!'

'Don't you mean "Anywhere?"

'Nope!' She sipped her wine.

'Relax!'

'I am relaxed!'

'No you're not! You're jumpy.'

'Well...I suppose I just haven't done this for a while.'

He smiled warmly and reached for her hand. 'Well...you're doing fine!'

She blushed. 'Look at you being so attentive!'

'We're not going to have an age related remark again are we?'

'My lips are sealed.' He sipped his wine. 'So...tell me more about you.'

She shrugged. 'Not much else to tell really.'

'I'm sure that's not true!'

'Well... just a single mum with her own company.'

'You said you have kids?'

'Well...they're not kids anymore.'

'So? Tell me about them!'

'Um...well...Ben's twenty-four; he graduated with a first in music - he wants to be a music therapist, and Rebecca is twenty-two, she wants to be an art historian.'

Admiration flickered in Jeremy's eyes. 'Wow! They sound amazing!'

'Yes! I just hope they stick at it.'

'In my experience...the older you get, the more mature and steadfast you become.'

'Not always!'

'Well...they sound great!'

'You'll have to meet them!'

'I'd really like that.' He raised his glass. 'To chance encounters.'

'Chance encounters.'

***

'I've really enjoyed tonight.'

'Yeah me too!'

She turned to him and smiled. 'You didn't have to come up to the door, the metre's running!'

He shrugged. 'So let it!

'Thank you!'

'For what?'

She blushed. 'This is only a first date...I shouldn't really say...'

'Nonsense! Say what?'

'Well...for making me feel alive I suppose...'

'You didn't need me for that, trust me...'

They looked at each other and the tenderness lingered between them, Jeremy broke the silence. 'Oh well...I should go....'

'Thank you for a lovely evening!'

'The first of many I hope.'

'For that cock-sure attitude young man, I shall screen your calls.'

He grinned. 'Well then you must forgive me for being so presumptuous.'

She suddenly kissed his cheek. 'Good night.'

'Good night.'

As Anna went inside and closed the door, she slumped against it, her heart pounding; she didn't have a clue what she was doing, all she knew was that she didn't want it to stop.

Chapter Three

Three weeks later

It was a gorgeous day and Jeremy had somehow persuaded Anna to come out for a picnic; they lay on the blanket as the birds and the sun shone down on them; it was pure bliss.

Anna smiled. 'I can't remember the last time I went for a picnic!'

'No?'

'No! Mind you, we hardly have the weather for it do we?'

'No, that's very true!' He sat up and grabbed the bottle. 'More fizz?'

'Oh I shouldn't!'

'Why? You don't have to work do you?'

'Well no but-' It was too late though, he had re-filled her glass. She smiled. 'Have you always been this forward?'

'Yes!'

She narrowed her eyes. 'I still can't believe you'd rather hang out with a dowdy middle-aged woman like me.'

'Well...As I've said, I want someone mature; I don't want someone who constantly lives in a rom-com.'

'Is that what your previous girlfriends have been like then?'

'There was this one girl who had to go into every wedding boutique we passed; she liked looking at the wedding dresses!'

'Well...a lot do that...'

'Yes, but they don't start discussions about hypothetical deposits for wedding dresses with shop assistants!'

'Ah!'

'Exactly!'

'...And how long, may I ask did these relationships normally last?'

'Well...my last one was just over a year...'

'Wow! No wonder she could hear wedding bells!'

'Oh don't *you* start!'

She laughed. 'Slightly OTT I must admit!'

'Yeah...exactly! I mean, I'm not adverse to getting married but I just want to take my time; not go at ten years per hour!'

'Well...as I've already said, that's very sensible! Marriage isn't all that it's cracked up to be anyway!'

He looked at her genially. 'No...I guess, sometimes, you can never really know someone!'

'That's what I tell my two! You can live with someone for years and discover some rather unpleasant surprises.'

'Are they still in contact with their father?'

'No, they hate him for what he did to me.'

'Well that's good!'

'In some ways...but, for all his faults... he *was* a good father to them.'

'Tricky!'

'Yes!'

He looked at her evenly. 'I bet you're a terrific mum!'

She laughed shyly. 'Well...I'm not really the person to ask.'

'Nonsense, anyone can see that!'

'Well...thank you!'

Suddenly his phone rang. He looked and then put it away.

'Important?'

'No, it'll be my mum. She can wait.'

'You can answer it; I don't mind!'

'No! No! She's just having these old family friends over for dinner and she wants me to be there.'

'Ah! The royal summons!'

'Yes, if you like!' She laughed. He frowned. 'What may I ask is so funny?'

'Nothing! Just..."Mothers & sons!"'

He laughed. 'Touché!'

They looked at each other, at first she felt shy, but the moment she looked into

his eyes and saw nothing but kindness
and warmth, she immediately relaxed.

He felt that he could lose himself in her
eyes; he felt hypnotised and couldn't
look away.

They both leaned in together and then
very, very slowly, their lips touched,
with the warm breeze, beautiful sunshine
and the birds singing, it was just the
perfect end to a perfect afternoon.

Chapter Four

Jeremy gave himself a last look in the mirror - he hated these dinners - but they were still old friends - he thought back to Anna, he would much rather be spending his time with her...she was so vivacious - he hadn't really met anyone like her, she was like a breath of fresh air - he was acutely aware of their age-gap and he didn't make that much of a habit of dating older women but when you clicked with someone, you just clicked! He wished she was coming with him now, having said that - this evening was going to be bad enough without being scrutinised.

...

He turned off the engine and looked at his parents' house; he sat still for a few minutes, composing himself.

'Hello Darling!

'Mum!'

'You look drawn; are you having enough iron?'

He fought the urge to roll his eyes. 'Yes Mother!'

'Right well come through!' Jeremy braced himself as he walked into the living room. He was met by beaming faces. 'Sue, Robert, you remember my son Jeremy?'

'Of course! And you remember our daughter, Jill?'

Jeremy smiled as a brunette approached him, smiling; she was attractive, just not to him.

'Hello Jerry!'

'Jill! Long-time no see!'

'Yes! When was the last time?'

'Oh must have been when we were about thirteen wasn't it?'

She laughed. 'Oh yes! You gave me a conker for my birthday.'

'Did I? That's me; always improvising!'

'I heard you're a curator in an art gallery now, that's impressive!'

'Yes! What do you do now?'

'I'm a cartoonist.'

He raised his eye brows. 'Really?'

'Yes, I'm not that good though it has to be said.'

'I'm sure that's not true!'

She laughed. 'Well...not really for me to say...'

...

The evening continued...but as it wore on, the more trapped he was beginning to feel; he knew perfectly well what his parents were up to...

'So Jeremy...how's your personal life?'

Jill groaned. '*Mum!!*'

Jeremy's mum shook her head. 'No, you go ahead! Maybe you'll have more luck! He never tells us anything!'

Jeremy shrugged. 'Well...I'm quite busy; I haven't really had any time to think about it.'

'I know the feeling!' Jill whispered.

He turned to her. 'I'm so sorry about all of this.'

'Me too.'

'It's been good seeing you again!'

'Same!'

'I'm sorry I pulled your hair that time!'

She laughed. 'Oh don't worry! It was years ago! I think I can overlook it!'

'Very generous.'

Finally the evening came to an end, Jeremy smiled.

'Well, it's been absolutely lovely to see you all again.'

'Ditto!' Jill's mum smiled. 'You must come to us!'

'Oh yes! We would like that!'

Jeremy groaned inwardly. The entire evening had been a set up and he knew it - he was tired and he was in no mood to discuss it now. As they were busy talking, he grabbed his jacket and tried to sneak out.

'Oh are you off dear?'

'Yes Mum, I have to, I've got a lot of work to do...' he didn't hear her say goodbye as he drove off, blood rushed through him, he was barely unable to contain his anger - could his mother *be* any more obvious? It was another attempt to try and control his life; his heart was pounding in his chest well no more... No. More. For once - he was going to do what *he* wanted to do... and no-one was going to stop him.

He pulled up outside her house and rang the doorbell.

'Jeremy!'

'Hey!'

'This is a surprise!' Anna looked at him concerned. 'Are you OK? How did the dinner go?'

'I don't want to talk about that.

Then, suddenly, he pulled her into his arms and kissed her deeply, something he had been aching to do all evening; she pulled away and looked at him before passionately reciprocating and pulling him inside.

Chapter Five

They just lay there for a while, staring up at the ceiling, suddenly, she turned her head.

'Where did that come from?'

He ran a hand through his hair. 'I have no idea...I guess I was just angry...I'm sorry, it's not fair on you' She stared at him and then laughed. 'What?'

'No, nothing!'

'No, seriously! What?'

'No, I just...I don't think I've met anyone as serious as you!'

'Don't you mean "Mature?"'

'No...'

He shook his head and grinned. 'May I remind you that I just arrived on a high of angry adrenaline to sleep with you?'

'Yes! You used me! How dare you!'

'You don't seem *too* upset by this!'

She stroked his hair. 'I am a forty-four year old woman - I'm not as sensitive as I used to be!'

'Fair enough!'

'But...you don't want to be tied down to a middle-aged frump like me!'

'Don't say that!' He sat up and cupped her face. 'You're gorgeous!'

'Did you get high before coming here?'

'I'm serious!'

She shook her head. 'You're strange!'

'Each to their own!'

'Why don't you give this other girl a try? What's her name?'

'I made it a policy not to become too invested in retaining a girl's name whom I have no interest in!'

'Ouch! That's harsh!'

'Better than stringing her along though wouldn't you say?'

'True! Very true!' She leaned down and kissed him slowly and deeply. 'Although...how do you know I'm not doing this to you?'

'Fundamental difference... I do know, she wouldn't!'

At that they both laughed and he wrapped her up in his arms with no desire to let her go.

****

Jeremy was busy cataloguing when his mobile rang. He frowned, not recognising the number.

'Hello?'

'Oh hello? Jeremy? It-it's Jill.'

'Jill! Hi!'

'Hi! How are you?'

'Fine! Sorry, how did you get this number?'

'Oh your mother gave it to me...'

Of course she did. 'Oh right!'

There was a pause. 'You-you don't mind do you?'

Mind? His mother giving out his number willy-nilly to anyone? 'No, of course not!'

'Well...great! I was just wondering if you fancied a really good catch up over a drink or a meal or something..?'

Jeremy paused, he couldn't string her along. 'Err... listen, you're really great!'

He could hear the disappointment in her voice. 'Oh...'

'Yeah, it's just that I'm sort of seeing someone.'

'Oh right! Your mother didn't say anything.'

'No, it's because she doesn't know...'

'Oh right!'

'It's just that she can be a bit of a micro-manager - and I like having a part of my life that's, well, private...'

'Of course! Well...I expect she's nice.'

'She is - in fact, she's amazing.'

'What does she do?'

'Oh she works in fashion.'

'Right...' There was a silence and he immediately felt sorry for her. 'I'd better go.'

'Well...take care and it was lovely meeting you!'

'You too!'

****

'Come on! Why won't you tell me?'

'Go away!'

'I won't until you tell me!'

'Don't you have work to be getting on with?'

'I will in a minute!'

Anna had popped into the office and was looking over some designs - her PA and friend, Polly, was intrigued by the spring in her step and was determined to find out why.

'Look, all I'm saying is, you've been coming in with a spring in your step lately.'

'Well...that's because I'm excited about the new lines which reminds me did you confirm our spot in Milan?'

'Yes! That's all taken care of!'

'Hopefully next Spring will happen.'

'Well...yes...hopefully, especially with the vaccinations. Anyway - you're changing the subject!'

'Oh I'm so sorry! There was my thinking you were paid to actually do some work!'

'Look, just give me something!'

'He's a little younger than me...'

'How much younger?'

'Double figures...And that's all you're getting!'

Polly gasped. 'Anna Martins you brazen hussy!'

'That's all you're getting!'

'We'll see!'

'Look just get back to work will you?'

She laughed. 'Alright! Alright! I'm going! I *will* say this though; he must be worth it if he makes you smile so much.'

Anna just smiled to herself as her PA left.

Chapter Six

'I shouldn't eat so much!'

'Don't be silly Darling! You're not fat!'

'No...not much anyway!!'

'Oh shut up you!'

'Ben, stop annoying your sister please!'

****

Jeremy had had enough sitting in the office and had decided to go out for lunch; it was a gorgeous day so, he left his jacket and strolled outside, he breathed in the fresh air and smiled as he enjoyed the sun shining down - suddenly, he looked across and saw Anna with two young adults, they must be her children. He watched them and felt warm inside as they talked and laughed, he was hesitant as to whether to just stroll over there and introduce himself, finally, he just decided to walk by and leave them to it, he didn't want to disturb.

Anna suddenly looked up and saw Jeremy walking by, she paused and looked at her children; unsure whether or not to beckon him over but then she strengthened her resolve...why shouldn't she?

'Jeremy?! Jeremy?!'

He suddenly glanced up and then after what seemed to be a pause, he made his way over. Although he had heard a lot about her children, suddenly seeing them sitting there in the flesh...made him nervous.

He approached them and smiled warmly. 'Hi!'

Anna beamed. 'Hi! Err...These are my children, Rebecca and Ben.'

'Hello!'

Rebecca beamed. 'Hello!'

Ben, on the other hand, was looking at him more cautiously, suddenly Rebecca hit him. 'Um...hello!'

'Nice to meet you both!'

'Join us!'

'Oh no! I should...'

'Oh please!'

Jeremy smiled. 'Alright, just a coffee then...' He sat down. 'So...I've heard a lot about you two!'

'Oh god!' Rebecca groaned. 'What's Mum been saying?'

'Oh it's all good I assure you! She's told me you want to be an art historian? That's really interesting!'

'Yeah, I just found myself intrigued by art in general and then I wanted to know more about the origins and that's how that started.'

'Wow! Interesting! And Ben, you want to be a music therapist is that right?'

Ben narrowed his eyes. 'Yes...what of it?'

'Nothing! I think that's very admirable.'

'Well...thank you for your input!'

'Ben!'

Jeremy shook his head. 'It's fine...don't worry about it!'

In the end, they spent an enjoyable afternoon - laughing and talking...well...*most* of them did; Ben just sat there, sullenly, he just couldn't take to him, he didn't like or trust him, he didn't know why...he just didn't.

****

'What is your problem?'

'What do you mean?'

Rebecca had stopped by Ben's flat. She took off her coat. 'You know what I mean! You were really rude today!'

'I'm not in the mood for a lecture from my little sister!'

'Well...tough! You're going to get one!'

'Look...I just don't like him!'

'What is your problem? You've only met him for five minutes!'

'Oh *please!!* Can't you see what's happening?'

'What...aside from you acting like a spoilt brat? No, not really!'

'Mum is having some sort of break down!'

'She *what??*'

'Isn't it obvious? This is all Dad's doing! He treated her like dirt, so now she feels she has to compensate by trying to make herself feel younger by going out with younger men!'

'Sorry...when did you suddenly obtain a degree in psychology??'

'Oh come on sis! It's obvious! She's making a fool of herself!'

'According to who...you??'

'Look, I just don't like or trust him?'

'Yes, I'm hearing this, but you haven't yet given me a valid reason!'

'Oh please! His age for one!'

'What's *that* got to do with it??'

'He could be our older brother! It's icky!'

'Oh don't be so stupid!'

'I'm sure it's illegal!'

'He's over sixteen! Don't start quoting things you know nothing about!'

'Either way, she's acting no better than Dad did!'

'How on *earth* do you work that out?!'

'Well...she's making a fool of herself! cradle-snatching virtually!'

'Oh don't you dare! You don't have a *clue* what you're talking about!'

'I bet he took advantage of her!'

'*What??*'

'Well...why else would he be interested? He probably thought that she was rich!'

'Oh and that's the *only* reason why anyone would be interested in our mother is it?'

'No, I'm not saying that!'

'Oh really? So what are you saying? Because, all I've heard so far is a string of insults! Grow up Ben! Mum can see who she likes and I'm happy for her!' She grabbed her coat. 'I'm not listening to any more of your rants just because your ego can't take it!'

'This has nothing whatsoever to do with my ego, all I'm saying is Mum's making a fool of herself by going out with someone who people will most likely mistake for her son!'

Rebecca threw open the door, ready to storm out...only to find their mother, standing on the doorstep...the hurt in her eyes told her that she had heard every word.

Chapter Seven

Jeremy tried desperately to phone her again for the umpteenth time; still nothing. He just sat in silence - feeling numb.

***

'Hello Mum!'

There was a silence, then. 'Hello dear!'

Ben felt a pang of guilt at how miserable she sounded. 'Is everything alright?'

'I'm fine dear! How are you?'

'Um...fine! Look, why don't I take you to lunch?'

'Take me to lunch?

'Yes!'

'My goodness! You MUST be feeling guilty!'

He was taken aback by how cold she sounded. 'Mum...I'm sorry...I-I was only thinking of you!'

'I know dear! Some other time though...perhaps.'

'Well...if you're sure...'

'I am.'

****

Ben sat in silence, he knew that he had been utterly selfish - he wanted his mum to be happy - of *course* he did; he was just unsure why someone so young would want to be with his Mum - it wasn't as if she had a lot of money! Maybe he could find out - amongst everything - he seemed to remember which art gallery he worked at.

Jeremy was closing down his computer and was about to lock up when he heard a noise. 'Hello?'

Suddenly Ben appeared. 'Hi!'

'Ben! This is a surprise!'

'You remember my name?'

'Of course! What can I do for you?'

'Can we talk?'

'Yes! Of course! Let's go to the Cafe...they always let me have a last drink before going home.'

They sat in silence for a while, Ben stared down at his coffee for a while - then he looked up.

'What *exactly* is your deal?'

'Excuse me?'

'With my mum?'

'No deal...I just really like her.'

'Do you have a "mother complex?"'

'Meaning?'

'Did your mother abandon you or something?'

'No...in fact the opposite, she can be a bit over-bearing!'

'I bet she doesn't approve of you and my mum!'

'She wouldn't be too thrilled that's true!'

'And that doesn't stop you?'

'Why should it? I'm an adult and my private life is my affair, no one else's, just like your mother's is hers...'

'You don't have to tell me that!'

'Don't I?'

'No! God! You really think you know it all don't you?!'

'I didn't say that! Look...I know you've had it rough.'

'What do you know about it? What do you know about *anything??!!*' Ben was embarrassed to realise that tears were rolling down his face, he then felt an arm go around his shoulders and he just cried and cried.

Chapter Eight

Anna was starting dinner, suddenly Rebecca came in. 'Still nothing from Ben'

'Oh he'll come.'

'I hope so darling!' She smiled sadly. 'I understand it was a bit of a shock...'

'Mum, you seriously don't want to listen to Ben - it doesn't matter what he thinks!'

'But it does! You two are both the most important people in my life; I want you to be happy!'

'Mum, you've thought about us your whole life; it's time to think about yourself for a change.'

****

'Here!'

'What's this?'

'A mocha, you need the sugar.'

'Thanks!' Ben looked at him warily. 'So...what's the deal with you two?'

'Well...as I've already said...I just really like her, she's a very special person your mother.'

'So you're not...'

'What?'

'Well...'

'After her money?'

He blushed and looked down. 'No, I mean I don't mean...'

'If I was, I would be getting her to buy stuff for me right, left and centre and I certainly wouldn't be hanging around...'

He just nodded in silence.

'Look, I'd best get off.'

'Wait! Why don't you come home with me? I know Mum would want to see you...'

'I can't, I've got a lot of work to do, tell your mum I'll call her.'

****

'Well, I hope you're happy!' Rebecca fumed.

'Look, don't keep on!'

'Don't keep on?! You've just cost Mum her happiness!'

'He said he'd call her!'

'Oh wake up you idiot! That's something blokes just say! Doesn't mean they'll actually do it!'

'He will!'

'Well, you'd better hope so mate, because if he doesn't...you'll pay for your petulant attitude!

Chapter Nine

One day seemed to roll into the next; Jeremy hadn't contacted her, and, to begin with, she wondered if it was to do with the fact that he wanted to give them space. Maybe it was for the best, except, she was discovering that she was missing him, she hadn't felt this happy in years and yet it was to be all taken away from her.

****

'You're very quiet Mum.'

'I'm alright Darling!'

'You're not!' Rebecca frowned. 'This is all Ben's fault!'

'Look, I said I'm sorry!'

'You can't blame your brother!'

'Yes I can and I do!' Suddenly, her mobile rang, they both stared at it,

Rebecca grabbed it and looked at her excitedly. 'It's him Mum! It's him!'

Anna felt her heart lift as she took the phone.

'Hello?'

'Hello? Anna?'

'Hi!'

'Hi!'

Both Rebecca and Ben smiled at each other.

***

'Well...that was unexpected...'

'Yeah!'

They both lay in bed; Jeremy rolled over and slipped an arm around her waist. 'I've missed you.'

'Me too!'

They both slowly began to kiss and explore each other's mouths slowly, enjoying every moment, he kissed her chest and she arched her back then he kissed her neck.

'I'm glad you came back...' He whispered.

'Are you really?'

'Absolutely...'

'I'm sorry; I ignored you...I just...well after his initial reaction...'

'Hey...I understand! It's fine!'

'I'm going to tell her...'

'Who?'

He turned to her. 'My Mum!'

'Slow down!'

'Sorry! I will though!'

She snuggled into him. 'Let's just enjoy the moment.'

They slowly kissed.

****

'Are you sure this is a good idea?'

'Absolutely! A month is long enough! I can't carry on with my mother trying to set me up; I can't keep stringing them along!'

'Do you want me to come with you?'

Jeremy paused. 'Actually...that wouldn't be a bad idea...'

'Round your place?'

Errr...no...Somewhere public, somewhere she can't make a fuss.'

'Scaredy cat!'

'You really don't know her!'

...

Jeremy glanced nervously at his watch.

'Stop worrying! It'll be fine!'

'Yeah! I hope so! You look gorgeous by the way!'

She blushed. 'Don't overdo it!'

They were sitting in the shopping centre outside a cafe, it wasn't too busy and Jeremy had thought it a good idea, somewhere public...with witnesses.

'Do you want another coffee?'

'I'm still drinking this one, just relax!'

'Yeah! Plenty of witnesses if the worse came to the worse!'

She laughed. 'It won't be as bad as that!'

Suddenly, he spotted a familiar figure. 'Oh god!'

'It'll be fine!'

'Yeah! That's what *you* think! Mum!'

She turned and waved as she made her way over. 'Oh hello dear! Sorry! It's very busy here today isn't it?!'

Anna nodded. 'Hard to park!'

'Yes! Oh I always come up here on the bus.'

'It's just easier isn't it?'

'Yes!'

Jeremy's mouth suddenly felt dry. 'Can I get you a drink Mum?'

'In a minute dear! Aren't you going to introduce me?' She smiled. 'I'm Jane and you must be Anna's big sister!'

Anna had to fight hard to keep a straight face.

Jeremy cleared his throat. 'Actually Mum...this is Anna...'

Anna turned to face Jeremy's mum, the look on her face said it all.

Chapter Ten

Anna had never known such a tense moment; the atmosphere could be cut with a knife, still, she tried her best to remain friendly, she smiled.

'It's very nice to meet you Mrs Fields!'

She just stared at her. 'Likewise.' Was the icy reply.

'So...Jeremy says you work in fashion.'

'Yes...in fact I have my own fashion brand!'

'Indeed!'

Mrs Fields sniffed and sipped her cappuccino. 'Yes, well, I don't know about you but I don't approve of cheap labour - all that working in sweatshops...'

Jeremy glared at her.

'Oh neither do I - everything is made in the UK and I'm quite selective and not very big.'

'Expensive?'

'Well...yes!'

Jeremy decided to jump in. 'She's brilliant! She holds fashion shows in Milan.'

'So!' Mrs Fields pressed on. 'Have you ever been married...Anna?'

'Mum!'

'It's alright! Yes, yes I have, I'm divorced.'

'Children?'

'Two, one each.'

'And what do they do?'

'Well...Ben; he's my oldest - he-'

'And your other?'

'Oh, Rebecca.'

'How old are they?'

'Well...Rebecca's twenty-two and Ben's twenty-four...'

'I see!'

There was a tense silence. Anna smiled. 'Well, I'll be back in a minute... excuse me.'

As she walked away, Jeremy glared at his mother.'...Mum, you are bang out of order!'

'*I'm* being out of order??? You've met someone to be old enough to be...well me!'

'Oh for god's sake Mum! How many twelve year olds do you know who have had kids??'

'It happens and that's not the point!'

'I really like her!'

'Look, when you're fifty...you'll be pushing her around in a bath chair!

'At sixty-two?? Oh stop exaggerating!'

'Look, she's a divorcee with two kids barely younger than you are!'

'What's that got to do with it?'

'You're only thirty-two! You've got your whole life ahead of you!'

'Mum! We are both consenting adults!'

'Oh and you want to be a step-father to two adults more or less your *own* age do you? You want to be tied down?'

Look Mum, I've had enough of this! It's MY life, I'm an adult and I'll see who I like and for your information; she is the most beautiful, *mature*, hard working woman I've ever come across and her

kids are great and if you don't like it,
then tough!'

It was then that they both turned round to
see her standing there.

Chapter Eleven

'Come on! Come on! Pick up!' Nothing, Jeremy had been trying for days but still nothing, shaky tears rolled down his face. How could his mother do this to him? How could she wreck the single best thing that had ever happened to him? The phone just rang and rang.

****

'Why don't you talk to him Mum?'

'No, Darling. It's for the best!'

'Oh come on Mum! How can you say that?'

Anna looked at both of her children and just smiled. 'When I was talking to his mother I suddenly realised that she was right; I *was* holding him back!'

'Well he didn't seem to be complaining!'

'No I know but he's twelve years younger! I can't do that to him! I'm just holding him back!'

'Mum! Where's this coming from? You were so happy!'

'I know...But it's over...there...enough...'

'What *actually* happened Mum?'

'Well...nothing...it was just his mother; she...said some things that made a lot of sense...'

'Oh *did* she?! Well, we'll see about that!' Before she could stop her, Rebecca had grabbed her coat and stormed out.

****

'It was nice today really wasn't it Darling?'

'Yes Mum!'

She smiled and took his arm. 'Spend some time with my boy!'

'OI! YOU!' They both turned round to see Rebecca run up to them, fuming.

'I'm sorry! Can we help you?'

'Who the HELL do you think you are??'

'I really don't...'

'What *right* do you have to dictate to *my* mum who she can and can't see?'

'Ah! You must be the daughter!'

'Don't patronise me you controlling bitch!'

His mother turned to him. '*Lovely* family!'

Jeremy stepped in. 'Mum, Rebecca, why don't we just calm down?'

'Calm down...*calm down???* She made Mum feel awful!'

'Well, maybe if your mother acted her age once in a while she wouldn't feel the need to demean herself!'

It all happened so quickly, Rebecca slapped his mother across the face as hard as she could before turning round and walking away.

'Did-*did* you see what she just *did* to me!!!! *DID you??!!!*'

Jeremy was utterly dumbfounded...yet, it had had an extraordinary effect, it was as if freezing cold water had been poured over him, allowing him to finally wake up from his mother's controlling ways.

'JEREMY????!!!!!'

He turned to her. 'I'm sorry Mother, I love you but, you deserved it - you have *no* right whatsoever to control my life; I see who I like and that's the end of it!'

****

After seeing her safely back and calming her down, Jeremy grabbed his coat and rushed round to Anna's.

'Alright! 'Alright! I'm coming!!!' Anna opened the door. 'Jeremy! What do you want?'

'You!'

Before she could reply, he swept her up in his arms and kissed her deeply, she wrapped her arms around his neck and hungrily reciprocated; she wasn't at all sure if this was going to be her happy ending...but, in that exact moment and time, it certainly felt like it.

Part Two

Part Two

Chapter Twelve

Two years later...

Jeremy sat in the car, waiting anxiously.
Every now and then he looked around,
worried that someone would see, that
someone might suspect something, he
looked anxiously at the clock and then he
looked across the street; still nothing,
there was nothing but darkness, he
looked at the house, a light was suddenly
switched on, he tightened his hands that
were around the steering wheel,
suddenly, a car pulled into the driveway,
his heart started to pound as a woman got
out and headed towards the house.
Suddenly, to his immense relief, he saw
a figure emerge from the bushes not far
from the house and run across the road; it
jumped in next to him.

'Well? Don't just sit there! Go! Go!
Go!!!!'

Exasperated...he pulled away from the curb and sped away. 'Nice evening dear?' He inquired sarcastically.

Rebecca gave him a pained look. 'Oh don't be like that!' He glanced at her. 'He told me he was single!!'

'Yes! Most philanderers do!'

'Well how was I supposed to know? I'm not psychic am I?'

'What have your mother and I told you about the "gift of the gab?"'

'I know! I know!'

'Your mother said he was too good to be true and...'

'...And I didn't listen yes I know!' She turned round and looked behind her. 'Phew! I got away with it.'

'What about his poor wife?'

'I swear I wouldn't have gone near him if I had known!'

'Poor woman!'

'Yes! Alright! You don't have to guilt trip me!'

'Alright! Alright!'

'How's Mum?'

'Worried!'

'Yeah, well, you can tell her it all went well can't you?'

He glanced at her. 'I think you're missing the point!'

'I'm not! I'll be more careful in future.'

'Just...remember sometimes it's the quiet ones who are the keepers.'

She smiled. 'Like you and Mum?'

'Yes! Well...touch wood!'

He pulled up outside her flat.

Rebecca gave him a big kiss on the cheek. 'Thanks Jerry! You're a star!'

'Any time! Perhaps next time you can climb out the window...mix it up a little?!'

'Ha! Ha! You're funny!'

'Just try and keep our blood pressure down alright?'

'Yeah! Yeah! 'Night!'

'Good night Bex'

****

It was late when he got back, suddenly feeling drained, he switched off the engine and sat in the driveway for a bit before heading inside.

'I'm home!' He smiled as he was greeted by the smell of Lasagne.

'Hi Darling! Dinner won't be long!' Anna came out wearing an apron and kissed him.

'Smells delicious!'

'Thanks! How did it go?' She looked at him anxiously.

'All sorted! I'm pleased to report that your daughter is safely back at home with no injury.'

'Oh you *are* good!'

'No problem! What are pseudo-stepfathers for?'

'I still can't believe she could be so stupid!'

'Well...the way *she* puts it; he came across as single - he was very charming!'

'Aren't they always?'

'I know! That's what I said!'

Jeremy set the table and Anna brought out two hot plates. He smiled and slipped his arms around her waist. 'You're amazing! You know that?'

'What about you? You're so good to us!'

'Hey! Come here!'

****

That night, as they lay naked in each other's arms, Anna sighed.

'I am worried though.'

'Hey!' He kissed her shoulder. 'They'll be fine!'

'Will they?'

'Yes!'

'Well...we've got Rebecca running around with married men! Ben, I don't really know what he's up to these days!'

'Look, they'll sort themselves out alright? And if not...well...that's what they've got us for! To help them pick up the pieces!'

'Yeah! You're right!'

He smiled and tightened his arms around her as they both drifted off to sleep.

****

It was dark...too dark...but the two figures didn't seem to care about that, one of them sighed.

'I'm not sure I can do this!'

'Yes you can!'

'There must be another way!'

'There isn't! It'll work out, I promise.'

There was a pause. 'Yeah...yeah you're right...Of course it will.'

Chapter Thirteen

'Are-are you sure?'

'Positive!'

Ben stared at his long term girlfriend, Wendy and glanced at the pregnancy test in her hand. 'I-I'm going to be a dad?!'

She nodded and grinned. 'Yes!'

He grabbed her and swung her round and round in his arms with her laughing.

****

It was night time... everywhere was cold and still, two figures sat in a car together.

'He bought it?'

'Yes!'

'Right!'

'I'm not so sure about this!'

'Look! We want the money don't we?!'

'Well...yes!'

'Well then!'

****

'So...come on! What's your big news?'
Jeremy had agreed to meet Ben for
coffee.

'I wanted to tell you first...because...well
you have always had a calm demeanour.'

'I'm flattered.'

'I know we haven't always seen eye to
eye...but you make Mum happy and I
appreciate that.'

'Well...that's nice to know...thanks.'

'OK, so I need you to break something to
Mum for me...'

Jeremy raised an eyebrow. 'OK...I'm guessing this isn't good...'

'Oh it is! At least *I* think it is!'

'Riiighttt.'

'It's just that Mum might freak out!'

'OK...'

'Lucy's pregnant!'

Jeremy spat out his coffee.

'I know!'

He stared at him. 'She's *what??*'

'She's pregnant!'

'With your child?!'

'Yes of course!'

'Right...'

'Don't sound *too* thrilled will you?!'

'No, it's just a surprise that's all!'

'I know! It's amazing!'

Jeremy sipped his coffee, trying to form his words carefully. 'And...you feel ready for this do you?'

'What do you mean?'

'Well...having a kid is a big responsibility Ben! I mean there are a lot of things to think about!'

'I can't do any worse than my dad did though can I? I just have to take on board what he did and do the opposite!'

'My understanding was that him being a father wasn't the problem.'

'Oh yeah! Because sleeping with someone else and walking out on your family really screams "dad of the year" doesn't it?!'

'Touché!'

'So...will you talk to Mum?'

'I'll try!'

Chapter Fourteen

'Rebecca...can I have a word?'

She groaned inwardly as she got up from her desk. '*Yes!*' She headed into his office.

'Sit down please!'

'What's this about then James?'

'Well...there's no easy way to say this...but we've been looking at the figures and we're going to have to make some redundancies...

Rebecca stiffened. 'Right...where is this going exactly...not that I don't already know...'

'Look...you're amazing! You really are! But we have to cut costs and...'

She jumped up. 'No need to explain; if you don't mind...I won't work my notice, I'll make it easier for you!' With that...she stormed out.

****

'I'm not sure about this you know...'

'It'll be fine! You always do a lovely shepherd's pie!'

'Not that you idiot!' Anna rolled her eyes. 'I meant these new lines for the show! It's so soon!'

'Look, if they've been given the go ahead then don't look a gift horse in the mouth!' He sighed, suddenly remembering his promise to Ben. 'Anyway...we have more important things to think about...'

'Oh?'

'Yeah! I think you had better sit down...'

'What's happened?' a look of worry appeared in her eyes.

'Well...it concerns Ben...'

'Oh Lord! What's he done now?'

'Well...'

Suddenly, the doorbell went.

Anna frowned. 'Who could that be?'

'Oh hello darling! What's happened Pet??!!'

Jeremy frowned as Rebecca suddenly came in. 'Bex! Hey! Hey!' he got up to give her a hug. 'What's happened?'

'I-I've lost my job! I'm being made redundant!!'

'Oh my Darling! No!'

Just as all this was going on, a text from Ben came through;

Have u told her yet?

Jeremy groaned; he certainly picked his moments! Still, one thing at a time...

'Oh there! There Darling!'

He handed her a drink. 'Did they say why?'

She sniffed. 'Just-just "last in, first out" more or less! What am I going to do?!'

'I know you did Darling!' Anna sat next to and put her arms around her. 'This is so unfair!'

'Yeah!' Jeremy added. 'But don't worry! You'll find something else!'

'In *this* climate?'

'I know Bex…' He refilled her glass.

'I mean! I *loved* that job!'

'And there's no room for negotiation?'

'No! They just said that they needed to make cuts!'

Anna put her arm around her. 'Oh Pet! I'm so sorry! But you mustn't give up!'

Jeremy put a banana split in front of her. 'Here! This always cheers you up!'

'Oh great! Get fat! Yeah that's the solution!'

'You always have this when you're down!'

'Touché!' She grabbed a spoon.

Jeremy shook his head...what with one thing and another!

****

'Poor Bex!' After she'd gone, Anna began serving up their dinner.

'Yeah! Loads of people in the same boat!'

'Yes! Maybe I could find her something?'

'You think?'

'Well...I've got a few contacts.'

Anna kissed him slowly and deeply.
'You are such a lovely man!'

'Well...I don't get that every day!' His
smile faulted. 'Listen! I know you need
more worry like a hole in the head but
there *is* something else you need to
know....'

'Oh god! Now what?'

'It concerns Ben...he confided in me and
wanted me to break it to you gently...'

'What on *earth* has he done now?'

'Well...his girlfriend's pregnant.'

She stared at him. '...Is-is this some sort
of *joke??*'

'Afraid not...he wanted me to tell you...'

'Oh! I see! I'm *that* much of a dragon am
I??'

'Darling of *course* you're not!'

'*How* could he be so stupid?!'

'Well...it's as much her as him!'

Anna re-filled her glass. 'What the hell is happening with those two?!'

'Hey! Hey!' Jeremy massaged her shoulders and kissed her neck. 'We'll sort it...don't worry!'

Chapter Fifteen

Rebecca scrolled through the job listings...she had already received several rejections and was quickly running out of ideas - she really didn't want to go to her mum for a job - she wanted to be as independent as possible. It had been a few weeks since she had been told to look for another job. It was a glorious day and she was sitting outside a cafe with a cappuccino and a large slice of chocolate cake.

'May I join you?'

She suddenly glanced up to see James. 'No, not really!'

'Look!' He sat down regardless. 'I'm sorry OK?'

'I'm not interested! Just leave me alone!'

'Look, it wasn't my decision!'

'Oh *really??*

'Look...Rebecca listen! You are terrific!'

'Yes! So you've said... look, just be straight with me alright? What is it...money??'

He stared at her and sighed. 'Partly! Like everyone...we're struggling a bit and cuts have to be made!'

'You sound like the government!'

'Touché!'

'So...what are you saying? Last in first out?'

'Well...I wouldn't put it *quite* like that...'

'Oh really?'

His eyes flashed and he sighed, exasperated. 'Alright! Fine! You want to know why I chose you? You're not the easiest person to get along with...'

'*Excuse* me??'

'Look...there *have* been times when you have been...well...to put it lightly...animated...'

'Well...that-that's just because of deadlines and people not doing their jobs properly!'

'Yes...but there are ways of doing things...'

She shrugged. 'So...that's it?'

'I'm sorry Rebecca!'

'...So am I!'

****

'I'm not a kid anymore!'

'No-one's saying you are dear!'

'Look mate... all we want to know is that you've really thought about this.'

Jeremy, Anna & Ben were all having lunch together and Anna and Jeremy had decided to stage an intervention.

Anna sipped her wine. 'Having kids is hard work!'

'Sorry Mum!'

'Oh Darling I didn't mean it like that!'

'Yeah! Your Mum and I just want to make sure you're aware of what's involved...not that I can talk!'

A small smile tugged at Ben's lips. 'Look, I know what's involved...but we really love each other! I'm going to look after both of them!'

Anna and Jeremy exchanged concerned looks.

****

Lucy glanced at her watch, she nervously looked up and down...wondering if he was even coming.

'Hey!'

'Oh Hey!' They kissed.

'I'm sorry I'm late...'

'No! Not a problem!'

Ben bit his lip. 'I just needed some time to think...'

'And???'

'Well...it's not going to be easy but...I'm in, I want to be there for you and the baby...'

'Ben... don't say it if you don't mean it...'

He took her hand in his. 'I do...one hundred percent!'

She kissed him happily.

'Look, let's go to dinner! My treat!'

'No, I'll pay half and that I insist on!'

'You're a hard woman to negotiate with!'

'Like you didn't know that already?!'

'So...pick you up around seven?'

'Absolutely!'

'Here!' He reached in his pocket and gave her fifty pounds.

'What's this for?'

'A head start...'

'Oh no...Jerry...'

'No...*listen*...we've got to make a start...just take it...'

'OK! Thanks!'

'See you later!'

They kissed and she watched him leave...waiting...she waited a bit longer then, putting the money away, she rushed round the corner where a car was waiting...quickly...she got in.

'Did he buy it?'

She got out the cash.

'Nice one!'

She bit her lip. 'I'm not sure about this!'

The man stroked her stomach. 'Look, my wages have been cut...we can't afford this on our own...so, this is a practical solution!'

'What....find a mug and rip him off?'

'Couldn't have put it better myself!'

She bit her lip. 'But-but what if he finds out?? What if-'

Hey! Hey!' He slowly kissed her. 'It'll be fine...trust me...the way this is going...we'll be set up for life.'

Chapter Sixteen

James didn't know what had got into him recently...he was unable to concentrate...he kept looking at the empty desk where Rebecca used to work...he shook his head...it had been the right thing to do! He had made an executive decision and that was it...wasn't it?!

****

'We'll have to get a pram and a cot...'

'Calm down! We've got ages yet!'

'Well...you know that time flies! I just want to look after you both!'

She smiled and stroked his cheek...'You do that and more!'

Ben nodded. 'Yeah...I just want to make sure...'

'Shhh....it'll be fine...'

****

James drove, looking at the house numbers; finally, he found her flat and drew up outside... He had no idea why he was feeling so nervous; he had made an executive decision! Yet no matter how many times he told himself that; it didn't change that fact that...here he was...driving through her neighbourhood at night...wanting to apologise. Finally, he came to her address.

'Oh! It's you!'

'Hi!'

Rebecca glared at him... 'What do you want?'

'Look...can I come in?'

'You've got a bloody cheek!'

'Look...please! I won't be long...'

She glared at him and then allowed him to enter. 'I'd offer you a coffee but I'm sure you're not stopping.'

'Look, maybe there's something I can do...'

'Don't bother!'

'No, wait! I can change your job title or offer you another position...'

'Don't you dare patronise me you creep!'

'Fine! That's the last time I try to help you!'

'*Help* me??? You were the one who took my job away from me in the first place!!!'

'Not through choice!!!'

'So... it *was* last in first out, as well as being...what was it you said...hard to work with?!!'

'Oh come on! Look, I *am* sorry about that part but you were hardly last in!!'

'Look...just go! Get out!'

'OK! Fine! Sorry I bothered!'

'I'm sorry as well!'

'Not even an expensive dinner? To apologise??'

She stared at him. 'I wouldn't go out with you if you were the last person on earth!'

'Fine! Not even Florentino's?'

'I-what?'

'Florentino's.'

She stared at him. 'That-that's the most expensive, prestigious restaurant in town!'

'I know! You can legally fleece me as much as you want.'

'Wh-why would you do that?'

He shrugged. 'Perfectly selfish reasons I can assure you; I gave a voucher to the last person I laid off...just my way of softening the blow, get me off the hook slightly...'

Suddenly it clicked. 'Hang on! Pete's birthday bash a couple of years ago!'

'Exactly!'

She stared at him. 'You're insane! Why not just allow them to keep their jobs?'

'Because a one off payment isn't the same.'

'Hang on...did you *plan* all this???'

He rolled his eyes. 'Yes! I'm a clairvoyant! No of *course* not!!'

She just stared at him.

'Look...I'll pay!'

'I must be insane!'

'Great! Friday? About seven?'

'*You're* paying mate!'

'Of course, that's what I just said!'

'Whatever!'

****

'So...how long do I have to keep this up?'

'Just a few more months babe, then we'll be off.'

'And what...I just disappear?'

'No! Then you tell him the truth!'

Lucy bit her lip and then kissed him deeply. 'This had better be worth it!'

'Oh it will, trust me!'

Chapter Seventeen

'Right! It's ready!!!' Anna called out.

Jeremy took the plates and put them on the table as Ben and Rebecca sat down.

'Thanks Mum!'

'So!' Jeremy poured out four glasses of wine. 'How's it going?'

Ben nodded. 'We're talking things through.'

'That's good.'

Rebecca frowned. 'Seriously Ben! You think you're ready for something like that?'

'What's *that* supposed to mean??'

'I'm just saying...'

'Alright! Alright you two!' Anna added. 'Calm down!'

Jeremy, sprinkled parmesan on his meal. 'Just take it slowly... don't rush into any decision.'

'A bit late for that!'

'Bex!'

'I'm just saying!'

'I know! I know what I'm doing...I'm fine!'

'OK! We'll leave it like that.' Jeremy sipped his wine. 'What about you Bex...any joy on the job front?'

She shook her head. 'Not really but I had a weird encounter with James.'

Ben frowned. 'Your ex-boss? What did *he* want?'

'Well...he sort of asked me out...'

'What did you say??'

'Well...yes...I suppose!'

Anna raised her eyebrows. 'Where's he taking you?'

'Florentino's.'

Jeremy whistled. 'He *must* be feeling guilty!'

'I know!'

'He fancies you doesn't he?'

'Oh don't be silly Ben!'

Her brother grinned. 'Seriously though! Why would he bother?'

'To soften the blow and to keep up his image...he's done this sort of thing before...'

'Yes but never one-on-one...'

'Ben! Pack it in! It. Is. Not. A. Date!'

'If you say so sis!'

****

It was a beautiful day and Jeremy had popped out to run a few errands...as he drove along, he suddenly spotted Lucy walking along...he smiled and was about to drive up and say hello...when he suddenly saw her greet someone. He stopped the car and watched them both intently for a moment or two...they seemed to be more than just friends...he watched her body language and then...to his disbelief...he saw her kiss him on the lips. He froze...maybe he had it wrong! But no, they were kissing properly. His head was spinning as he thought about how excited Ben was. He couldn't ignore what his instincts were telling, *screaming* at him; that his pseudo-step-son was being taken for a mug; what was he to do now?

Chapter Eighteen

Anna smiled as she looked through the latest designs; these were exactly what she had been hoping for; Milan was four months away; it had been decided that it would go ahead but it had to streamed online because of the pandemic which was a shame because she had been hoping to treat them all to a family holiday; still, a lot could change in four months it had to be said.

'Hello Darling!' She smiled as Jeremy came in. 'There's some wine in the fridge.'

'Great! Thanks!'

'Whatever's the matter?

He calmly got out the rosé and poured himself a glass. 'I've just witnessed something.'

'What?? An accident??'

'No...no! Nothing like that...' He sat down. 'I saw Lucy in town today...she was with this guy...'

'So?'

'They-they looked very friendly and then...then I saw them kissing...'

Anna stared at him. 'What...kissing him on the cheek?'

'Yes Anna! Come on! Do you *really* think I'd be like this if it was just a peck on the cheek?'

'You-you're mistaken!'

'Am I?!' With that, he produced his phone and showed her the photo.

She stared at it and then put a hand to her mouth.

****

Rebecca straightened up and looked at herself in the mirror; for the umpteenth time, she wondered why she was doing this...still...she got a free dinner so she couldn't really complain! Suddenly, she heard the doorbell go...after a last look; she took a deep breath, grabbed her bag and went downstairs.

James raised his eyebrows when he saw her. 'Wow! I mean...good evening!'

She smiled. 'Good evening!'

'You err...You look great!'

'Thank you!'

'Shall we?'

****

'You're sick! You know that?!'

'Ben...look, just listen to me-'

'No! I mean what *is* your problem?'

'Look, I don't want to see you made a fool of!'

'NO? Would that be because you just want to cause problems??'

'BEN! How can you say such a thing? He wants to help??!!'

'*Help?? HELP???* He just wants to cause trouble!' He turned to him. 'What's your problem exactly? I thought we were friends!'

'We *are* mate!'

'Friends don't do what you're doing!'

'And what am I doing exactly?'

'Deliberately trying to put a wedge between us! You and Mum have never liked the idea!'

'That is NOT *true!* Your mum and I are just worried that-'

'Well *save* it!!! I don't need you two interfering, and, at least MY relationship

is a lot less controversial than
YOURS!!!!'

'Look mate-'

'DON'T call me mate! Just stay out of
my life alright?!'

Anna's eyes flashed. 'You apologise
right now!'

'Why the hell should I?'

'Well...at least he cares which more than
your father ever did is!'

'Well...at least he didn't mess with my
life!'

'No! That's because he couldn't care
less!'

'Whatever! At least he was your own
age! I'm going to stand by her and our
kid – I've already set her up financially
with her own card and there's
NOTHING you can do about it!'

With that, he stormed out without looking back, leaving Jeremy and Anna to look at each other, alarmed.

Chapter Nineteen

'Wow! This-this place is nice!'

'What did you expect?'

'I don't know! Mind you...if you're trying to butter me up then you're going the right way about it!'

He laughed. 'Call this an "apology dinner!"'

'I thought it was a "get you off the hook" dinner.'

'Can't it be both?'

'Touché!

They were shown to their table. 'This doesn't change anything!' She warned.

'I know! I'm sorry! It was just...'

'I know...you don't need to repeat it.'

James shook his head. 'Oh god! This isn't easy for me...'

'What?'

'I wasn't *exactly* planning on firing you...'

'*Excuse* me?'

'I had a plan; fire you from your current job...and then re-hire you; simply under a different job title...'

She stared at him. 'How was that *ever* going to work??'

'Oh please! They don't pay attention! They just want the figures to add up!'

'That's dishonest!'

'Yeah...I know...I'm sorry...'

'And that's supposed to make everything better?'

'That *is* the general function of an apology!' Her mouth twitched. 'Hey! Was that a smile?'

'You wish!'

'I think that was a smile!' He teased.

'Oh shut up!'

'Look, your job is waiting for you if you want it.'

Rebecca shook her head. 'I should sue you for psychological damage!'

He raised his eyebrows.

'I mean why would you still want me around anyway?'

'Beats me! You're infuriating, you *never* do as you're told...'

'Oh don't stop! I can *never* have enough compliments!'

'Anyway...I'm really, *really* sorry!'

'That's not the *point!* These are people's *lives* you're messing with and you just don't seem to care!'

'Well…that doesn't mean I don't want to…but…at the end of the day… I *am* running a business and I just can't *afford* to…I've got people on *my* back as well you know!'

'Yes! Paying you a nice, fat salary…'

'That's as may be but, trust me, they want their pound of flesh!'

'Well…at least you're honest!'

They looked into each other's eyes a little longer than they were supposed to, she looked away first.

'Anyway...'

'Yeah!'

Having cleared the air, they both had an enjoyable evening in the end and when it came to pay the bill; Rebecca got out her purse.

'Hey! Hey! You're not paying!'

'Don't be silly! The least I can do is pay half!'

'No! Absolutely not!'

'Oh but I insist!'

'Well...I insist harder!'

'Well...take it out of my severance pay, I won't be held to blackmail!'

'Oh *that's* not melodramatic is it?!'

She shrugged.

He laughed. 'You won't give way with this will you?'

'Absolutely not!'

'Fine!'

'Good!'

'Look, I *am* sorry about your job...I'll see what I can do.'

'Look...don't do me any favours... I don't need to be patronised!'

'Oh my god! You are so-'

'Exasperating? Infuriating? Yes, you've said!

****

Rebecca smiled as he saw her to the door.

'Well...I suppose I should thank you for a lovely evening, surprisingly!'

'Yes...the tiny bits where we weren't arguing!'

She shrugged. 'Well...what did you expect?'

True!'

'Still, my mother taught me to be polite so...thank you.'

'My pleasure!'

'You know, can't *actually* believe I'm saying this but...you're not as bad as I thought!'

'Well...thank you!'

'Are you sure you won't come in?'

'No, I'm sure thanks!'

'Well...thank you and good night.' With that, she kissed him on the cheek and headed inside.

She went inside and closed the door...smiling to herself.

****

Meanwhile James' mobile rang; he glanced at the number before answering it. 'All sorted; she won't be any trouble now.'

Chapter Twenty

Jeremy sat staring into the distance...worrying about Ben; he couldn't just stand by and watch him be ripped off. Suddenly, he had an idea, slowly; he turned to the computer and began typing.

'Jeremy! This is a surprise! Did Mum send you?'

'No! I was just in the area and I wanted to apologise.'

'Really?'

'Seriously mate! We were both out of order and we're pleased for you.'

'If this is some sort of joke...'

'Not at all mate!'

Ben narrowed his eyes at him. 'Well...come through!'

'Thanks!' Jeremy quickly looked through Ben's coat pocket and found his wallet, then, he slowly swapped his card for the pre-paid one he had just bought.

****

'I've got a surprise for you!'

'Oh don't tell me... a pram?'

Ben laughed. 'I'm not going to rush you into anything! But...here...'

'What's this?'

'A card to my personal account! Knock yourself out!'

'What?'

'Look, when I said I wanted to look after you two...I meant it! I love you.'

'Happy tears came into her eyes. 'I-I don't know what to say...I love you too.'

They hugged and she pushed the card deeply into her pocket.

****

Anna glanced up and smiled as Jeremy came into her office. 'Hello Darling! What a lovely surprise! What are you doing here?'

'Well, I was just passing and I thought that I would take my wonderfully, talented woman to lunch.'

She kissed him. 'That sounds lovely! I just grab my bag!'

'So...how's it going? Are Vogue begging for an inside scoop yet?'

'Oh it's not funny to make fun of me!'

He laughed and kissed her.' Trust me Darling! Anyone who has achieved what you have does definitely not deserve to be laughed at!'

'That's sweet!' She kissed him.

'Wow! That was nice!'

'I'll pay!'

'Don't be silly! We'll go half!' After signalling for the bill, Anna smiled. 'So...how's Ben?'

Jeremy kissed her hand. 'It's all sorted, don't worry!'

'What about-'

'It's sorted, I promise!'

She sipped her coffee. 'I *know* they're not kids any more but-'

'You're their mum; it's your job to care!'

'Yeah! I know!'

'Everything's going to fine! Trust me!'

****

Lucy was feeling more and more confident. 'Look what I've got!' She sang as she got through the door.

'More clothes?'

'Kev! LOOK!'

He glanced up and saw her waving what looked like a credit card...

'Oh my GOD! You- You ACTUALLY did it!'

She giggled and nodded.

'Oh come here!' He swept her up in his arms and swung her round and round.

****

'You look studious!'

James suddenly looked up and saw Rebecca, smiling at him. 'Oh! Rebecca! Sorry! I was lost in my thoughts.'

'Yes! I can see that!' She sat down. 'Anything interesting?'

'No! Just boring paperwork!'

'Do you even *know* how to relax?'

'Now...I think that's *very* unfair!'

She laughed. 'I've seen you and your working lunches!'

'Yes well, I have to keep things afloat!'

'I refer you to my previous question!'

'Yes! I do as a matter of fact!' He paused. 'I just...haven't had much of an opportunity...'

'Come with me!'

'Where are we going?'

'You'll see!'

****

'The number you have called is not available...please hang up and try again.'

Ben frowned and tried again, same problem. He shrugged...there was sure to be a perfectly rational explanation!

****

'Thanks for this!'

'My pleasure!'

'I can't really remember the last time I just relaxed!'

'Well...there you go!'

He sighed. 'Look, I know that I'm a workaholic!'

'That's an understatement!'

'I just...there's always *something* to do!'

She smiled. 'Why do you find it so hard to relax?'

He shrugged. 'I don't know! I just...one job rolls into another and, before I know it, I'm on a conveyor belt.'

'Well...you should learn to hop off it occasionally!'

He laughed. 'You're right...again!'

'I usually am!'

'He smiled at her. 'Why did I let you go again?'

'Cost-cutting wasn't it?'

'Amongst other things!'

She smiled.

'What?'

'No, nothing!'

'No, come on! What is it?'

'No, it's just…it's just you're so different from what you're like in the office.'

He laughed. 'Yes! I have two identities!'

'Clearly!'

They both stared at each other, both sensed the chemistry between them yet, neither seemed willing or brave enough to make the first move.

Chapter Twenty-One

'The number you have called is not available...please hang up and try again.'

Ben frowned and tried again, same problem. He shrugged...there was sure to be a perfectly rational explanation!

****

'What do you *mean* the card's not working??'

'Just what I said!'

'It must be!'

'Well...it doesn't!'

He snatched the card and looked at it. '*You stupid cow!* Did you even *look* at it properly?? Did it *ever* occur to you that this is a *pre-paid* card??'

She stared at him. 'Wh-what do you mean??'

'I mean we've been had!'

'We-we *can't* have been! How would he know?'

'Well he *obviously* found out!'

'But-but I've been so careful!'

'Well...*clearly* not careful enough!'

'Kev! Kev wait!' She rushed after him...unaware that Ben had been watching from afar...

****

'Hey James!'

'Rebecca! This is a nice surprise!'

'You don't know what I'm going to ask you yet...'

'True!'

'Look...just a quick bell to check that you're OK to provide me with a reference?'

'Of course! You've found something then?'

'Yes! Not to brag but it's the Glower Art Museum.'

He paused. 'Wow! That-that's on the other side of town...'

'Yeah! I know that it'll be a bit of a trek but that's why I'm moving...'

'You-you're moving?'

'Well...yes! I mean the amount it would cost me in petrol.'

'...Yes...I suppose so...'

'So...you'll give me that reference then?'

'...Yes...Yes of course.'

'Thanks!'

'No problem! Good luck!' He hung up...wondering why he felt as if there was a knot in his stomach.

****

Where could he go? He felt so humiliated! He had been taken in - he sat there and thought about how he had been so excited and taken in by her lies. He felt sick; finishing off his fourth large bottle of beer, he grabbed his coat and car keys.

****

'Thanks again for doing the dishwasher! You always do it better than I do!'

'I know you're only trying to butter me up!'

'Am I *that* transparent?'

'No! I just know you too well!'

She laughed as he handed her a glass of wine and sat down next to her; she tenderly stroked the back of his head. 'What have I down to deserve you eh?'

'Thanks a lot!'

'You know what I mean!'

'Hey! You've all had a rough time, you deserve some happiness.'

'We don't deserve you!'

He laid a hand on her thigh. 'Yes you do...'

She smiled as he slowly began to kiss her, his hand moved up to her waist.

'Actually...there-there's something I've been wanting to ask you...'

Her heart fluttered. 'Yes?'

'Well...'

Suddenly, there was a knock at the door.

Anna frowned. 'Who could that be?'

'I'll get it...' There, on the doorstep was Ben, it was obvious he'd been drinking. '*Ben!!*'

'You were right.' He collapsed into Jeremy's arms and started to cry. 'You were right.'

Chapter Twenty-two

Jeremy and Anna lay in bed the following morning.

'I can't believe it! You're so, so good to them, you really are!'

'It was nothing.'

'Don't say that! She could have cleaned him out!'

'Yeah! Well...she didn't!'

'Thanks to you! I wouldn't have thought of that!'

He kissed her shoulder and then slowly worked his way downwards...she closed her eyes and a slight moan escaped her lips

'What were you going to ask me?'

Slowly, Jeremy pulled her closer and slipped his tongue in her mouth. 'I think you know...'

She closed her eyes as she felt a million sensations rip through her body. 'Yes! Yes, I will!'

****

'Ready to go?'

'Rebecca grinned. 'You don't have to keep treating me to breakfast!'

'I know I don't but I want to!'

'Honestly! Why are you doing this?'

James swallowed. 'Honestly? I'm not sure...'

She smiled and then pulled him in for a kiss; he froze before slipping his arms around her and hungrily kissing her back, something that he had been wanting to do for ages.

****

Ben was staring into his coffee, Anna and Jeremy came down the stairs and she placed an arm around his shoulders. 'Did you manage to get any sleep darling?'

He shook his head. 'Not really!'

'Hey!' Jeremy clapped his shoulder. 'Don't worry mate...we've got you, all of us!'

Anna grabbed the phone. 'I'll call your sister. We should all be together at a time like this.'

'Oh yes! Thanks Mum! Let's increase my humiliation!'

'Hey! *None* of this is remotely funny and it could happen to anyone.'

'But it didn't did it Jerry? It happened to me!'

'You're definitely not the first and you certainly won't be the last! This is the problem with classic stereotyping! Everyone assumes it's the bloke! So much that women tend to slip under the radar.

****

Rebecca heard her phone, she slowly reached for it.

James kissed her shoulder. 'What is it?'

'It's Mum.'

'Everything alright?'

'No...it-it's Ben...the woman he was with tried to rip him off!'

James stared at her. 'For how much?'

'Thousands!

'Dear god!'

'I can't believe it!' She got out of bed. 'I-I've got to get going...'

'Do you want me to come with you?'

'No! No that's fine!

Suddenly his phone went, he sighed and went to reach for it; he knocked it onto the ground. She bent down.

'Oh no! Don't!'

'No! No! That's OK!' She bent down and grabbed his phone but froze when she saw the text.

Kept her sweet about the severance pay?

She stared at him. 'What is this?'

James paled. 'Look...it's not-'

"Kept her sweet about the severance pay?" What does *that* mean??'

'Listen-'

'Were you *trying* to cheat me out of what I deserved??!!'

'No! It-it wasn't like that!!'

'Oh *really?*'

'Look...I knew you wouldn't give up and we're struggling financially!'

'So...what? You decided to treat me like a mug?!'

'You *were* going to get severance pay!'

'...Just nowhere *near* the amount I needed or deserved!'

'Rebecca! *Listen!!*'

'No! Wh-what did you think?? That you could *sleep* with me and that would be it??'

'No! No! Of *course* not!!!'

'You must have thought me a right slut!'

'Rebecca! *Please!!* Yes...alright! It-it started out like that! I knew how strong willed you were and I thought you would cause trouble for the company and when I saw you I was only trying to be nice and then...I admit it...I thought I could use it to my advantage; but I was wrong! I had no right! I didn't plan for it to happen but it did! I fell in love with you!'

'Oh! What's this??? *More* severance pay?'

'Look! I'm sorry alright! The-the company hasn't been doing that well and so we had to cut costs.'

'Why the *hell* didn't you just *say* that??'

'Because I knew you would think it was just an excuse!'

She looked at him...tears in her eyes. 'If you knew me at all...you would know that I would have appreciated it more if you had just been honest with me.'

With that she left, leaving an atmosphere of heartbreak behind her.

Chapter Twenty-three

'I don't think we should tell them just yet.'

'I agree!'

Jeremy and Anna glanced at them, glumly at the kitchen table with a mug of coffee. They looked up as they entered and forced a smile.

'Thanks for letting us stay...'

'Yeah...thanks.'

'Oh nonsense you two!' Anna replied as she kissed both her children. 'This is your home! You stay as long as you want.'

'Right!' Jeremy turned to the cooker. 'Who fancies a big, unhealthy fry up?'

'It's not Sunday!'

'So? We're a day early, besides...you two need cheering up!'

Ben and Rebecca looked at each other and smiled slightly. 'Waffles *and* sausages?'

'You've got it kiddos!'

Rebecca sighed. 'We're hardly kids anymore!'

Jeremy sighed. 'Alright!!! Sorry!!' He was smiling though and she managed half of one back.

'Oh my Darlings!' Anna reached for their hands. 'It'll all be fine in the end...'

'Mum...what's that?' Ben was staring at her hand.

'Oh...that...'

Rebecca's eyes widened.' Oh my god Mum! Are you two..?'

Anna paused. 'Oh no...I meant to take it off! I completely forgot!'

Jeremy went over to her and put an arm around her shoulders. 'Sorry! We meant to tell you when things were a bit happier...'

Ben and Rebecca looked at each other, smiled and then hugged both of them. 'It's great news! Congratulations!'

'Wow! Thanks! Are you sure?'

'Absolutely!'

'Even you Ben?'

Ben smiled. 'Jerry, you've been more of a father to me than my own father *ever* was!' He paused. 'Maybe "father" is a bit too much; older brother!'

'Good to know! Thanks!'

'Well...' Rebecca grinned. 'What are we doing? Let's crack open the champagne!'

Anna paused. 'Do you know? I think there *is* a bottle somewhere...'

'I'll get it!'

As Rebecca grabbed a bottle, she heard her phone go; she saw a text from James.

Please can we talk?

She put her phone away and went back inside.

Ben looked a little shyly at Jeremy.

'I-never properly thank you for-'

'Oh don't be silly! It's what *any* step-father would have done!' He frowned. 'How did you know?'

'Well...the penny dropped when she started yelling at me that I had given her a pre-paid card...'

'Oh yes! That reminds me...' He got up and came back in with his wallet, he handed him the card. 'I think this is yours...'

Ben stared at it then; he slowly picked up a pair of scissors before cutting it in half.

Suddenly Rebecca returned.

'Everything alright Darling?'

'Fine Mum!' She smiled. 'Absolutely fine.'

Chapter Twenty-Four

A few weeks later...

Rebecca was busy replying to an e-mail when she suddenly heard the door go; sighing, she got up to answer it and was amazed to find James standing on the doorstep.

'What do *you* want?'

'Can I come in?'

'Sure! Oh wait! Shouldn't you have an ulterior motive or something?' She asked sourly.

'Please! We need to talk!'

'I don't think we have anything to say to each other!'

'I think we do!'

She looked at him, uncertainly. 'You've got five minutes!'

'Thank you.' He stepped inside. 'Have you had any luck finding something else?'

'A few offers doing temporary work but nothing major.'

'Oh, before I forget...this is for you.' He handed her an envelope.

'What's this?'

'What you're owed; it's all there.'

'Oh! Thanks!' Suddenly, she ripped it up. 'You can't *buy* me!'

'It's what you're owed!'

'Well...I resent the implication!'

He stared at her then shook his head. 'Well...that's not really my problem then!'

She went white. 'How...*dare* you! After everything *you've* done!'

'Look! I've said I'm sorry alright?'

'Oh that makes up for cheating me out of *my* money does it?'

'Fine! I admit! I'm a selfish bastard who couldn't really care less! But I didn't plan on falling in love with you!'

She stared at him. 'What did you say?'

'What?'

'Just then!'

He paused. 'I've fallen in love with you. I miss you, I stare at the person who's at your desk and I wish it was you alright? That's why I quit! Not because I could find something better but because I'm sick of the atmosphere and I'm sick of being a puppet on a string, being bullied into *being* the bully myself!'

She stared at him.

'Anyway, that-that's all I came to say...I'll leave now.'

'Wait!'

He turned and they stared at each other before she wrapped her arms around his neck and kissed him deeply, he wrapped his arms around her waist and reciprocated.

Chapter Twenty-Five

'I love this material Mum!'

'Yes! It *is* lovely isn't it?!'

'Oh god! You two aren't *still* at it are you??'

'Ben! This is Mum's *wedding!* It's not just *any* old thing!'

'Oh it's only *Mum's* wedding is it?' Jeremy came in, looking amused. 'I'm glad someone told me!'

'Sorry Jerry! Just saying...'

Jeremy laughed and sidled up next to Ben. 'You alright mate?'

He managed half a smile. 'Medium.'

'Hey! You've absolutely nothing to be ashamed of.'

'Doesn't change the fact that I allowed myself to be sucked in.'

'Yes! You and thousands of others, that's what makes it such a lucrative business!'

'I just...I just thought that she really loved me.'

'Hey!' He put an arm around his shoulders. 'You're a great person and any woman would be lucky to have you.'

'Yeah! Right!'

'No! I'm *serious!* And one day...you're going to meet that special someone.'

'Like you and Mum?'

'Exactly!'

'Oh...by the way...'Rebecca sipped her drink. 'I'm bringing a plus one...'

Anna looked intrigued. 'Oh? Who?'

'James.'

The three of them stared at her.

'*James??*'

'Yep!'

Ben's eyes widened. 'When did *that* happen?'

'A few weeks ago!'

'Isn't it a bit premature then?'

'Oh very funny!'

Jeremy raised his eyebrows. 'Wow! You and James eh? Good for you!'

'Your life is just a Mills & Boon novel isn't it sis?'

'Ha! Ha!'

Anna laughed. 'Well...good for you Darling!'

'Anyway! This is about Mum and Jeremy!'

'Hear! Hear!'

'Cheers!'

'Congratulations Mum!'

'Congratulations Jerry!'

Anna smiled. 'Here's to the future!'

'To the future!'

Chapter Twenty Six

'They're so happy aren't they?'

'Yeah! Well...if anyone deserves it, they do!'

'Absolutely!'

'He's perfect for Mum, I've never seen her so happy!'

Rebecca narrowed her eyes. 'OK! Who are you and what have you done with my big brother?'

'Yeah! Alright! I admit I had my reservations at the beginning...'

'That's *one* way of putting it!'

'Oh god! I'm sorry!'

'What for?'

'For not being the big brother I should have been?'

'Don't be stupid!'

'No! I'm serious!' Ben sat back in the chair. 'I'm your older brother, I should have been supporting you rather than being wrapped up in my own problems!'

'It's not like it was anything *minor*! You thought you were going to be a dad for god's sake!'

'Yeah! Look how *that* worked out!'

'Well... you *were* seeing her! It's not like she came out of no-where!'

'Yeah! I don't know what I would have done if Jerry hadn't been there...'

She grinned. 'We've come such a long way haven't we?'

'Yes!'

'I mean I remember when you *hated* him!'

'Hate's a bit strong...'

She laughed. 'Oh my *god!!!* You were convinced he was after her money!'

'Yeah! I know! I think it was just reality hitting me you know? That Mum and Dad were completely finished and weren't getting back together.'

'Yeah! I know, but then again whose fault is that?'

'True!'

'It's worked out for the best though hasn't it?'

'Absolutely!'

'Cheers!'

She touched his glass with hers. 'Here's to new beginnings.'

'New beginnings.'

****

Eight months later...

'I think it's amazing Mum! You're getting married the same day you met!'

Anna laughed. 'I know dear! I couldn't believe it when there was a cancellation...'

Ben frowned. 'Why was it cancelled?'

'Oh they didn't say!'

'Probably ran off with the bridesmaid!'

They both sniggered.

'Hey! Behave you two! Anyway why is it always the man's fault?'

Ben shrugged. 'Why does it have to be the man who ran off?'

'Touché!'

'Anyway! Mum! Are we going to see this wedding dress today or what?'

'You two ready?'

'*Yes!!*'

'OK!' She threw back the curtain to reveal a stunning cream dress with a purple sash.

They both stared at her.

'What?' She bit her lip. 'Too much?'

'Mum! You look *gorgeous!!*'

'Really? You don't think it's too much?'

'Absolutely not!'

Ben kissed her on the cheek. 'Mum, you are a knock out!'

'Yeah! Jeremy won't know what's hit him!'

'Oh thank you, you two!'

'Here's to you Mum!'

'Here's to *all* of us!'

Epilogue

A year later

He was nervous; he couldn't pretend he wasn't...for the second time, he checked his watch and did a quick scan at the waiting guests.

'Stop fidgeting! It'll be fine!' Ben muttered.

Jeremy smiled. 'Thanks mate! You've got the rings haven't you?'

'No! I flogged them on E-bay!'

'Not the *best* time to crack jokes!'

'Sorry! Couldn't resist!'

The sun shone and there was a pleasant, cool breeze. Suddenly, he looked up and saw Anna coming down the aisle; she had never looked more beautiful.

****

Later, as they danced, Anna held him tightly.

'You showed up!'

He frowned at her. 'What's *that* supposed to mean?'

'I don't know! I suppose I just thought that all of this would put you off...'

'Put me off??'

'Yes!'

He frowned. 'Well...let's see...in the past year or so I've had to help your daughter escape from a house where she was having an illicit affair and the wife nearly caught her then help play matchmaker and save your son from being a victim of fraud.'

She bit her lip. 'It's a lot.'

'Yes! And I wouldn't have missed *any* of it for the world.'

CPSIA information can be obtained
at www.ICGtesting.com
Printed in the USA
LVHW030237250522
719632LV00004B/59

9 798201 755317